FAMILY

A REACHER SHORT STORY

L E FITZPATRICK

Copyright (C) 2014 L E Fitzpatrick

Layout design and Copyright (C) 2019 by Next Chapter

Published 2019 by Beyond Time – A Next Chapter Imprint

Cover art by The Cover Collection (http://www.thecovercollection.com/)

This book is a work of fiction. Names, characters, places, and incidents are the product of the author's imagination or are used fictitiously. Any resemblance to actual events, locales, or persons, living or dead, is purely coincidental.

All rights reserved. No part of this book may be reproduced or transmitted in any form or by any means, electronic or mechanical, including photocopying, recording, or by any information storage and retrieval system, without the author's permission.

Read more about L E Fitzpatrick

https://www.facebook.com/lefitzpatrickbooks

THE REACHER SERIES

The Running Game
Border Lines
Every Storm Breaks
Safe Haven
The Lost Shepherd

1

At the time, standing between a loaded gun and a life of hardship in S'aven, the Smith brothers seemed like a good option. It was only later that Rachel realised they were her only choice. She was a Reacher, able to read and manipulate the minds of others. And she was a wanted woman. The government would see her dissected. Criminals would put her out to work. She'd tried to live under the radar but they had found her. It was only a matter of time before it happened again. She had no choice but to run. So she ran. With them.

But the road ahead was dark and cold and dangerous. And the men she had thrown her lot in with were darker and colder and infinitely more dangerous. They barely spoke. The pair so accustomed to life together they didn't need to chat. Rachel had that once, when she travelled with her own family, fleeing war in Red Forest. Since then she lost her family. Since then she had been alone. So Rachel sat in the back of their stolen car, suffering the silence and listening to the doubts in her head.

What did she really know about them? The younger brother, John, was a ruthless killer. He'd dropped body after body with machine like efficiency and, not once in the time since, had he shown any remorse. And Charlie, well Charlie was even more broken; an addict sliding down a pitiful spiral of his own making. He was a Reacher, like Rachel, but his dependency on painkillers had rendered him close to useless. They came to her rescue but they weren't heroes. So what kind of men were they?

They were a day out of S'aven, cruising the back roads of the south of England, trying to lose any tails that might have followed them out of the shanty town. They had left a lot of bodies in their wake. Even Rachel had blood on her hands and, as the night started to break, she felt the ghosts of aging gangsters and dirty cops watching them from the open road. *The Running Game, that's what her father had called it.*

The surrounding countryside was desolate, made even emptier by the impending winter breathing an icy threat from the north. The temperature had dropped, green turning to grey. Every now and then another vehicle would pass, reminding Rachel that, despite the desolation, there was still life out here. At the sight of each set of headlights the brothers tensed. Rachel had grown accustomed to doing it herself too. There were rumours about the country-folk, and she was from the Red Forest in the north, she'd seen isolation turn reasonable people into raving lunatics.

In the back of their cramped car, Rachel huddled up as best she could. She was cold and hungry. A bag full of money occupied the space beside her. She owned a third share of the cash, more than she had ever had in her life, but she would have traded it all in for a thicker jacket and a protein bar.

"Open service station in fifteen," John said. "Car needs fuel."

"We need to stock up too. Might as well do it in one trip."

Outside faint rays of purple touched the barren landscape. Rachel couldn't imagine they would find food or fuel in a place like this. Then the small road widened. They passed another car and hit a crossroad. John took an immediate right, clenching the steering wheel as they hit a larger stretch of tarmac. The scenery opened up, scarred by the stretch of road running into the horizon. There were more cars in the distance, all moving at a fast, constant speed.

John's head lashed around. He slowed the car, hitting a steady fifty rather than matching the other vehicles.

"What's wrong?" Rachel asked, feeling the air in the car tighten.

"Nothing, John's just being over cautious," Charlie assured her.

"Are you going to say that when we get jumped by some inbred cannibal waving a machete?" John replied.

Charlie nudged his brother. He turned back to Rachel, forcing a reassuring smile. "Sometimes the motorways can be dangerous, especially the further away from London you are. There are police check points ever fifty or so miles but in between you get gangs and local authorities hijacking cars. Don't worry we're only jumping on to get to the services and they're pretty well protected. It'll be fine."

"That's what you said last time," John murmured.

"We're still here aren't we?"

"Give Rachel a gun."

"I'm not sure I want a gun," Rachel said.

But John was adamant. *He knows I've killed one man, he thinks I can do it again. Maybe I can.*

Charlie handed her a small black snub nose from the glove box. She stuffed it into her jacket pocket rather than hold it.

Smoke billowed from the hard shoulder. The air acrid and sickly sweet. As they neared, Rachel could make out a vehicle smouldering on the verge. The contents of the car had been ripped out and spread over the cracked tarmac. Clothes caught in the braches of the surrounding trees. Underwear. Jeans. A girl's dress. Rachel stared at the black lump of metal as they went past. A body smoked in the driver's seat, alone in a motor coffin. She touched the snub nose in her pocket.

The brothers didn't talk about it.

2

John pulled off the motorway towards a dirty brick structure, strangled by bramble bushes and litter. Six petrol pumps sat outside the building, beckoning the passing traffic. A spattering of white lights lit up the entrance to the building, the only indication the place was open for business.

"Let's make this quick," Charlie said. "I don't want to hang around here any longer than we need to."

John pulled up at the end pump. As he opened the door another light inside the service station ignited, illuminating an old man in a checkout booth, watching them through the protection of a mesh screen. Rachel could just make out his cold eyes, peeking out of a thick, knotted beard.

Another man came out of the main entrance. He was younger, the muscle of the setup, carrying an automatic rifle like it was baton. He wore an armoured vest, two sizes too small for him. It sat open, exposing all his vital organs.

"They look welcoming," John said.

"I guess they've been having some trouble. I'll go tell him we come in peace and everything should be fine." With difficulty Charlie got out of the car. He'd been stabbed in the back, suffering severe nerve damage in his spine and legs. He walked with a crutch and, when people saw him approaching, they assumed he was harmless. A fatal mistake.

John's focus intensified, concentrating on the men watching his brother. He was wound tight, ready to strike in a heartbeat if he needed to.

"Is it always this hostile?" Rachel asked.

"Sometimes. Winter makes people nervous and irrational."

"Is it so important we go inside?"

"We need supplies," John stated, still concentrating on his brother.

Neither brother seemed particularly worried. But something didn't settle well with Rachel. Before John could stop her, she got out of the car.

Charlie could move things with his mind, but Rachel had her own talents. She focussed her energy and slipped between the pumps. She moved behind Charlie, quickly catching up with him. He didn't notice she was there. *You can't see me, you can't see me.* The mantra repeated on a loop, making her invisible to the men around her.

The old man in the booth stood up, his hands concealed, likely holding a weapon. Charlie made sure his hands were visible. He smiled—not arrogantly or confidently—just appreciating the difficult situation and respecting it. Nobody even looked Rachel's way.

"Stocks are low," the old man said. "Things don't come cheap."

"I appreciate that, times are hard. As I said we need supplies for the winter. We'll pay whatever the asking price is. No haggling, we've got a long journey ahead, we just want to get going."

The old man considered it. He cast his eye over at his guard and then nodded.

"This place had a lot of trouble?"

"Trouble?"

"The security," Charlie said.

"Times are hard as you say," the old man said. "Got to keep our wits about us."

"All right if my brother fills up while I get supplies?"

The man nodded. The guard made no effort to move. He would watch John and make sure the fuel pumps were safe. Fuel was a commodity people couldn't waste anymore. Charlie gestured to his brother that they were good to go and headed into the service station. Rachel followed.

The door to the building was heavy, reinforced with steel and able to be barricaded from the inside. There had been windows, but these had long since been boarded up, barred like the door. The lights fizzed into life as Charlie entered, working off a motion sensor to conserve energy. Rachel waited until the door closed and touched Charlie's shoulder. He jumped.

"Jesus, what are you doing?" he said.

"Things don't feel right," she said. "Those guys out there…"

"They're taking precautions. It's a tense world out in the wild, you've just got to see it from their point of view. We show up, John glares that them, they're bound to be worried. But we'll give them a fair price, no trouble and everything will run smoothly. Don't worry. There's a canteen on the left, go grab something to eat."

"I thought we weren't staying long," she said.

Charlie put his hand on her shoulder and gave it a reassuring squeeze. "If there's trouble they'll put up the barricade. We'll be safe inside. This is a business, they need our custom as much as we need their supplies. They'll take care of us."

She stared at him, still unconvinced.

"Go get a coffee and relax."

He hobbled to the right, towards a kiosk selling basic supplies. The old man from the front was already opening up the shop, lifting the grates over the secured shelves for Charlie.

Rachel wanted to follow Charlie, but didn't. He was right, she needed to relax. Charlie and John lived their lives on the road, if they said there was nothing to worry about, she could ignore the unsettling churning in her stomach. This was all new to her, it made sense that she didn't feel safe. A couple of minutes with a hot drink and full belly would clear her head.

She pushed open the door to the cafeteria and stopped. The room was dark, dust clouds filling the beams of light from gaps in the boarded windows. There were booths along three walls, the fourth reserved for a self-serve buffet table, manned by an enormous woman slouching at her till counter, cigarette poking from her blistered lips spilling ash onto her yellow-stained apron.

There were others in the café. Three men talked loudly at the far corner. They looked like labourers, possibly farmers trying their hand at something new while the ground was too hard to work. On the left two other men huddled over a teapot, barely moving in the bleak light. They were well dressed, maybe travelling from one city to another. Near the door to the toilets a mother sat opposite her two young children, all eyes fixed on their untouched plates of toast.

As Rachel stepped inside the group of men stopped talking. The canteen fell into a tense silence. She wanted to make herself invisible, she wasn't even sure she could do it now they knew she was there. She swallowed her nerves and headed for the sanctuary of the buffet counter, after all she was just another diner seeking sanctuary for a few minutes.

Taking a battered plastic tray, she ran it along the buffet table. There were assorted pans of tinned foods, beans, canned meats, corn. The contents were stewed to thick brown pastes. It was the most appetising sight Rachel had seen in a long time. Her stomach growled and before she could stop herself she had a full steaming plate. She filled a cup of coffee from a dirty jug and scoped several heaped spoonfuls of sugar into it.

Two worn hands rested against the table beside her. "What's a pretty thing like you doing in a place like this?"

The man leaning over her had been cajoled into breaking away from his pack. He was probably not thirty yet but his skin was already tarnished and leathery, his hair thinning at the front and greying on the sides. He was wearing a thermal jumper over a pair of old jeans and smelt of smoke and oil. He grinned at her, exposing two rows of decaying broken teeth.

"By the looks of it I'm attracting unwanted attention," she replied, moving away.

He reached out to touch her and stop her from moving. She lashed around as his fingers brushed her arm. *Don't!* The words shrieked in her mind. It was enough. He backed away, a glint of fear and confusion in his eye. He didn't understand what had happened but he was scared. The other men jeered at him, but he wouldn't go after her again.

Rachel ignored them and took her tray to the fat woman at the counter. She was cackling along with the other men, spraying ash over the counter. Her fat fingers punched numbers into the till and she coughed out the bill. Rachel handed over the cash and winced when the woman stuffed the notes between her breasts.

Rachel chose a table away from the others. She sat so she could keep an eye on the room and watch the door. The group of men laughed again, their bellowing making the room claustrophobic. They were all armed, rusting guns stuffed in their belts.

Rachel put her first spoonful of food in her mouth, savouring the odd taste and texture. Her eyes drifted around the other customers. The two men, isolated by themselves had barely moved since she arrived. Rachel noticed their hands were squeezed together tightly. One looked at her. His face was bruised and swelling. His wide eyes seemed to scream at her in panic. It was then she noticed his partner and the pallid lifelessness of his skin. Her stomach lurched.

The fat woman waded across the dining room. She leaned over to the group of men. Whatever she said made the men groan. They waved her away, but it was clear they respected her—or at the very least were intimidated by her. As she shuffled away, heading towards the toilet, Rachel felt a hunger rise within the men.

While their attention moved to the man and his deceased lover, she got up herself. She concentrated with all her might. *You don't see me*, she thought, *you can't fucking see me so don't even look.* Her feet gingerly moved towards the door. Then she stopped. The family of three were sitting to her left. The youngest, a girl, was trembling. A pool of urine had settled beneath her shoeless feet. The family smelt of smoke and blood. Rachel reached out and touched the girl's head. Then she saw it. The burnt out car. The father consumed by flames. Bad men on the mother. The children watching. Unable to turn away in case they lost their only surviving parent.

She removed her hand, unable and unwilling to leave. She sidled into the family's booth and smiled at the shell shocked children. Their wide eyes took her in. Their mother watched the lard harden on her cold slice of toast. Rachel touched the children's hands.

"It's going to be okay," she told them, her words penetrating deep into their subconscious. Neither flinched when the gunfire started outside.

3

The last time Charlie had been on the road he was doped up on self-prescribed pain killers and in a bad place. His wife had been murdered, his daughter was missing, and, in a confused daze, he wandered the aisles of another service station, looking for supplies to keep him and John alive. Little had changed in the intervening months. His wife was still dead, his daughter still missing, and there was still a lingering trace of the narcotics in his blood stream.

Although, there was one difference. There were three of them now. Adopting Rachel had been a decision made out of circumstance and because of what she was. Just like him she was a Reacher and the bond between them was instantaneous. He couldn't allow her to be hurt, it went against every instinct he had, and leaving her in S'aven would undoubtedly have been leaving her for dead. People knew what she was, it was only a matter of time before they tracked her down and forced her to use her powers. It was only a matter of time before she got caught and killed.

Charlie watched Rachel disappear into the canteen. She was smart. And she was a fighter—she had to be. Charlie just wasn't sure if she was ready to fight his battles with them. And even if she was, he wasn't sure he wanted to burden her with the responsibility.

He went into the kiosk and reached for a basket. His outstretched hand was trembling. It had been over a day since he'd last taken his medication. He checked around and reached into his pocket to retrieve his pills.

"What's that you're taking?" The old man appeared at the till in the corner. "Tim, get over here, we've got a thief!"

Tim, an acne covered teen, was in the kiosk before Charlie could show them what he was hiding. The barrel of the rifle followed his hand as he removed his pills.

"Just getting my medicine."

Tim snatched them and tried to make out the label. He made Charlie turn around and checked his other pockets. He let Charlie go but kept hold of his pills.

"I need those," Charlie said.

"Then we can trade for them," the old man said. "Think of it as insurance. I'll be watching you."

"I told you, we don't mean you any trouble."

"If I had a pound for every goddamn thieving bastard that said that to me I wouldn't be sat here waiting for winter."

Charlie conceded the point. "I'll be as quick as I can."

He turned to the shelves. They were well stocked, not like most places this time of year. This station had everything they needed; protein meals, water purifiers, thermal clothing. Charlie started filling his basket. Then he stopped, midway through the protein meals.

"You got plenty of stock for the winter?" he asked.

"What's it to you?" the old man snapped.

"Just don't want to clear you out."

"There's no chance of that."

"Never seen shelves this full this time of year before."

Neither the old man, nor Tim, answered. *Things don't feel right.*

The world outside of S'aven was barren and wild. Things were different. People were different. And Charlie adapted accordingly. He'd suffered winters in the wilderness and bustled with the chaos of the city. He understood the service station, the caution they had towards him, the steps they would go to if they thought their lives or livelihoods were threatened. He respected them. But Rachel was right. Things didn't feel right.

Carefully, he put the basket of supplies down. He'd made a mistake. Rachel was in another room. John was outside. They should have stayed together. Charlie closed his eyes and listened. There was noise throughout the station; people, machinery, the hum of a generator keeping the place alive. They could easily be outnumbered. Service stations were normally well armed, with large store rooms potentially filled with guards. Charlie flexed his fingers. Things were going to get messy.

He turned to the old man as the sound of a vehicle shook the outer wall. The old man fought a smile, the hint of smugness betraying what was about to happen. Charlie shook his head.

"You can stop," Charlie told him. "You can call it off, we'll pay for what we want and leave without trouble."

"You don't do much steady walking as it is, I don't think we've got much to worry about."

Charlie smiled back. "Well it's not just me you have to worry about. My brother is not a man you should underestimate." Charlie paused, Rachel wasn't defenceless either. "Nor is the woman."

The old man's eyes flicked to Tim. He hadn't seen a woman.

Two shots fired outside. John had a rhythm Charlie would recognise anywhere. A car horn blared. Charlie stared at the old man. He raised his hands and the shelves lifted. The old man had enough time to draw his shotgun before the metal frames hurtled into him. He was pinned. His weapon out of reach. Charlie dropped to his knees before Tim could get a good aim. He swiped his crutch and knocked the rifle out of Tim's hand. But it was still strapped to the kid's shoulder and just spun around his back. Charlie dived at him, knocking him back into the corridor. The pill bottle hit the floor and shattered. What was left of Charlie's medication lost in the debris of the kiosk. The boy writhed underneath Charlie and Charlie lost his temper. He slammed his fists into the kids face, knocking him out.

Charlie rolled off the boy and shook the rifle free. As he tried to get up he felt the full force of the fight in his legs. The gunfire outside grew louder—something automatic. Charlie glanced at the exit. Help his brother or find Rachel? For a moment he was torn. Then the automatic firing stopped. Mind made up, he lunged towards the door to the cafe.

"Rachel!" he shouted as the butt of an identical rifle smacked him across the face.

4

John didn't like their car. The tyres were cheap, fine for city travel but no good for hitting country dirt tracks. He wasn't confident about the battery either. They were going into hibernation and the car was filled with useless gadgets which would drain the power in a week. It was Italian too. John was particular, he liked his cars German—everything else was only good for scrap.

He filled the car with petrol, watching as one security guard went in and was replaced with another. From where he was standing he could inspect the quality of their weapons. They were forgeries, probably good for a handful of shots and little else. It was easy to manufacture weapons for novice fighters looking to protect themselves. If a man wasn't interested in heavy duty a counterfeit rifle would do nicely, but John could see by the arrogance with which these weapons were being held that the shooters had no idea how lousy their armoury actually was.

The new guard leaned against the wall of the entrance. He was feigning disinterest in John, more fascinated in the floor than what was going on in front of him. He should have been more cautious. He should have been watching John.

The petrol pump clicked. The car was full. John opened the boot.

The movement drew the guard's attention but only briefly. His casualness was starting to annoy John. Even when John removed a petrol can from the boot the guard barely flinched. With a shake of his head John went back to the pump and started filling again.

A rumble struck the road into the service station. A concealed bend hid whatever was coming, but John knew it was big. He glanced up at the guard. He hadn't drawn his weapon, he wasn't even concerned. This was an ambush.

As the first glimpse of the Humvee came into view, John had already put the petrol can down and replaced the pump. If he ran, took out the guard at the door, he could make it into the service station. But what would be in there? And what vantage point could he take? The Humvee rolled closer. Six men inside and a mounted turret on the back. It was overkill and it was going to be their downfall.

The Humvee rolled towards the pumps. The men inside were cheering. These weren't trained killers, or even the wild men of the north intent on raping and eating anything that crossed their territory. These men had just been made desperate. Whether it was a failed delivery, or maybe a robbery that had seen their supplies dwindled, something had pushed these men towards drastic action. Their plan—and it was obvious to John—was to lure unsuspecting travellers to them and rob them for everything they had. John could see from the dark glint in some of their eyes that killing had followed as a consequence. These men were getting a taste for it. It would be a thirst they wouldn't have for long.

John moved quickly. His weapon was pointing at the guard by the door before the car stopped. The guard dropped, a hole in the centre of his head. John adjusted his position, calculating the next target. The driver's head hit the car horn. The Humvee rolled forward, hit the second petrol pump and stopped. The men inside were in shock. Two of their own were dead and they hadn't even made eye contact with their killer.

As they piled out of the vehicle, John was already moving. Using his own car for cover, he fired another two shots. One man flew back, punctured in the chest. The other clasping his neck as his jugular erupted in a fountain of blood. Then John ran. A volley of shots clipped the bricks of the service station wall, but John was already behind the corner. He flexed his shoulders and dared a look.

They were coming. Two of them. The youngest of the pack, taking brave steps towards the side of the building. Their breathing heaved under the pressure. Their footsteps crunching on the dirt. John counted. Six. Five. Four. One of the men was wavering. He slowed behind his comrade. Three. Two…

The gun came before the body. John snatched the barrel and slammed the weapon into the wall. Its owner yelped, fumbling for a hold on the weapon. John shot him in the chest, then turned the corner to deal with the coward.

The turret nearly caught him. He ducked back to cover as it ate up the tarmac. And then he heard it—a shout coming from inside the building. The turret stopped. It was his chance. He stepped out, grabbing the last guard on foot. He pulled him close, putting a bullet in his leg. The boy screamed, his writhing body was a perfect shield.

Holding onto him, John marched, seeking out the man operating the turret. Like a fool the gunman was standing upright against his machine gun, looking at John with a gaping mouth. It took one bullet to bring him down. John pushed the boy he was holding to the floor. He fired his gun again, putting a full stop to the bloodbath.

As he stepped over the body in the doorway, John's mind was already on clearing the inside of the building. He heard groaning coming from the kiosk. The noise coming from a pile of shelving. It wasn't Charlie or Rachel so John wasn't interested.

He turned to the cafe instead. When he kicked the door open he spotted Charlie on the floor. His brother was still breathing—John raised his gun—which was more than could be said for the men beating him. With the bodies fallen he bent down to lift his brother up. Charlie groaned.

"What the hell kept you?"

John looked around the canteen. A man for some reason sitting opposite a corpse, a woman sat with two shell shocked kids—nobody threating. John rested Charlie against the wall.

"You good?"

"Yeah, I'm great. Where's Rachel?"

Someone started wailing. A huge woman charged at them, a knife raised in the air. John went for his gun but a bullet fired before he even got it out of the holster. The woman thundered to the floor, crushing the bodies of the other departed men. Rachel stood behind her. The gun in her hand smoked.

"I'm here," she told them. "And when I tell you something isn't right, bloody listen."

5

Since meeting the brothers Rachel had killed twice. She didn't regret either death, maybe that was John's influence. This was how the world was now. And she was intent on staying alive and keeping the brothers alive—her brothers now.

They followed John out of the station. He pointed at the Humvee and the adorning corpses littering the vehicle and the carpark.

"Subtle," Charlie said. "And I bet you want to keep the turret don't you?"

John didn't answer—of course he did.

"Fine," Charlie conceded and left him with his new toy.

Rachel took the opportunity to check Charlie over. In her old life she had been a doctor and Charlie had never looked so much like a patient.

"Satisfied doctor?" he said.

"I think you'll live. Does it hurt?"

"Of course not," he lied.

She was concerned, he didn't need to cope with any more pain.

"I lost my medication."

Before he could protest she drew him near. "Then let me help." Pain and addiction started in the mind and that was her domain. She pushed an idea he could build on: *you can cope, you can do this*. When she pulled away he looked brighter. He didn't say anything, he just gave her a grateful smile.

"Are we really going to drive around in that?" she asked, nodding at the Humvee.

"John's got a thing about military vehicles."

"What about our car?"

6

The surviving diners pooled together instinctively, claiming John's discarded Italian car. Rachel and Charlie watched them leave the road with satisfaction. They took the rest of the supplies they needed from the kiosk and loaded the Humvee with anything else that looked useful. The old man still groaned underneath the shelving and he would until the cold or starvation caught up with him. Rachel helped load up the car and settled into the roomier backseat.

Rachel sat back and looked at the brothers, the bag of money by her side, now the least valuable thing she had with her.

Standing between a loaded gun and a life of danger on the road, the Smith brothers were a very good option. Maybe this new family could make it after all.

END

PREVIEW OF THE RUNNING GAME

Reacher Series #1

1

Five past eleven.

Rachel's shift should have finished three hours ago. She slammed her time card into the machine. Nothing. She gave it a kick, then another until it released, punching her card and signing her out for the night. The hospital locker room was unusually quiet. There was a nurse signing out for the night, two doctors signing in. Nobody spoke to each other—it wasn't that kind of place. Grabbing her threadbare coat from her locker, she drew it over her scrubs—the only barrier between her and the unforgiving October night. She walked through the ER waiting room, eyes fixed on the exit. You had to ignore the desperation. Three hours over a twelve hour shift, you had no choice but to pretend like you didn't care. Push past the mothers offering up their sick children like you could just lay your hands on them and everything would be better. Push past the factory workers bleeding out on the floor. Push that door open and get out. Get home. You had to. In six hours the whole thing would start again.

The first blast of cold air slapped the life into her aching body. The second blast nearly pushed her back inside. She tightened the coat around herself, but the icy wind still managed to weave its fingers through the thin material and loose seams. November was coming, and coming fast. She quickened her pace, trying to outrun the winter.

She hurried past the skeletal remains of another fallen bank, a relic of the days before the economy crashed and the country went to hell. Now the abandoned building housed those left to the streets: the too old, the too young, the weak, the stupid. Cops would be coming soon, moving them on, pushing them from one shadow to another until dawn or death, whichever came first. But for now they sat huddled around burning canisters, silently soaking in the heat as though they could carry that one flame through winter. They didn't notice Rachel. Even the most evil of men lurking in the doorways, waiting for helpless things to scurry past, overlooked the young doctor as she made her way home. Nobody ever saw her. At least they never used to.

Three – two – one.

Nine past eleven. Right on cue.

She felt someone watching her. It was always the same place, opposite the third window of the old bank. He was hidden, not in the bank but close. So close she could almost feel his breath on the back of her neck. She'd watched muggings before, these were desperate times and people took what they could when they could. There were rapes too, five this week, at least five that had needed medical care. It was a dangerous city and getting worse. But this was different. He—and for some reason she knew it was a he—did nothing. For a week he had been there, never betraying his exact position or his intentions, but she could feel him and the longer he waited the more he tormented her. He knew where she lived, where she worked, the route she took to the exchange store. And he escorted her home each night without ever showing himself. It made no sense. And that made it so much worse.

She wasn't intimidated easily; doctors in St Mary's couldn't be. It didn't matter that she was only five feet tall and looked like a strong wind would knock her down; she could still take care of herself. But the stalking had spooked her. The sleepless nights followed as she wondered who he was, what he wanted, if he knew.

There was nowhere for her to go in the city, no place she could hide, no escape. If she wanted to eat she had to work, and he would be waiting for her outside the hospital—watching, doing nothing. She was tired of it, tired of everything, but there was something she could do. She could make it stop, one way or another. Whatever he had planned, whatever he wanted to do to her, he would have to look her in the eye as he did it, because she was done running.

She stopped walking and turned.

The street was empty. But she could still feel him there. The buildings pressed their darkness into the street and the spattering of hissing lamplights did little to expose the nocturnal danger below. There was noise. There was always noise; voices, vehicles, the persistent buzzing of the electricity struggling to reach the edges of the city. So much going on, yet so little to see—a perfect place to hide.

"Okay you pervert," she whispered to herself. "Where're you hiding?"

The road stretched back into a tightrope. Gingerly, her feet edged back towards the ruined bank. She scanned the buildings around her, the upper windows, the ground level doorways, waiting for him to pounce. One step, two steps. Look. Nothing. She retraced her steps to the next building. Then the next. He felt so close—why couldn't she see him?

"You want me, well here I am, you freak. Come and get me!"

There was a shout from the bank. Someone running. A man. Her stomach clenched. She braced herself. He pushed by her, hurrying away. It wasn't *him*.

She turned, her eyes trying to make sense of what she was seeing. Then warm breath touched the back of her neck.

"Get down!"

The world went white.

With her face pressed into the filthy, cold road, Rachel waited. The ground beneath her trembled, but that was it. She frowned, waiting for something, trying to understand what she was doing lying in a stinking puddle at the side of the road. Hands were lifting her to her feet. She turned to the bank, but it was gone. Flames licked at the pile of rubble in its place. People stumbled from the wrecked building, choking and coughing, others with their eyes as wide as their mouths. But there was no sound, just staggered movement and growing heat. Rachel watched, feeling more curious than afraid. The silent panic was fascinating. She made to move and her ears exploded with noise. The shock of it knocked her back. Screaming, cries for help, the ringing of sirens came from every direction.

The ground shook again and the building exploded another mortar firework into the street. She felt her body being tugged away. But people were coming to help. People were still alive. She was a doctor, she was needed.

"I can help these people," she shouted trying to fight off the man holding her back.

"It's a lure bomb." The voice was so cool it made her freeze. She looked at the stranger and swallowed the clumps of gravel lodged in the back of her throat. She had wanted to meet him face to face but not like this.

He stared at her with blank eyes. The dead and dying meant nothing to him. He was there for her and her alone. His hand still held her shoulder, holding her back. The hand that had pulled her to safety. So many questions ran through her head but she could only push one out.

"A lure bomb?"

A small explosion that drew in the police, she raced to remember. *Followed by the bigger bomb that would blow them to pieces.* She turned back to the space where the bank should have been. More people were rushing to help, pulling at the arms and legs of the buried. If they were lucky bodies would come with them.

"We have to warn…" The man had gone.

The sirens grew louder.

Rachel drew in a steadying breath. *Three hours over a twelve hour shift – you have no choice but to pretend like you don't care.*

She started to run.

2

Charlie jolted awake in his chair, his face sodden with sweat. He wiped his forehead with his sleeve. Pain coursed up his back, reminding him of his nightmare. The recurring dream of the day it all went wrong. He fumbled through his pockets until he found his pills. The placebo was instantaneous, and the pain relief followed shortly after. He rubbed his eyes and returned to the camera positioned towards the apartment in the opposite tower block.

The lights were on, curtains open. Someone had come home and he'd missed it. His one job and he'd screwed it up. He kicked out at the crutch resting against his chair and watched as it skidded across the floor out of his reach. Flexing his hands he willed the crutch back to him. Nothing happened.

"Shit."

He lifted himself from his chair too quickly and his right leg buckled, knocking over the camera – only the most expensive bit of kit they owned. The lens cracked.

"Shit, shit, shit." He shouted from the floor. The shockwaves of pain started to subside. Anger and shame fought their usual battle, while the voice inside his head urged him to just quit already. And, as usual, a persistent nagging from his bladder brought everything into perspective. He carried a lot of indignity on his shoulders, the last thing he needed was to be found sitting in a pool of his own piss.

This wasn't how his life was supposed to be. Charlie Smith had been a legend. He was a Reacher, born with incredible powers and an arrogance that made anything possible. With his former self firmly in his mind, he rested his head on the floor and focused on the crutch again. His fingers stretched out, reaching for the plastic handle in his head. He could still sense the weight and feel of it with his powers, but to move it took an effort his brain struggled with. This should have been easy but his telekinetic powers were failing him. The camera shook, turned on its side and then stopped altogether. The effort was exhausting and embarrassing.

Slowly, because nowadays everything had to be done slowly, he edged himself over to his crutch and, with it in hand, he managed to make it to the bathroom. It was a small victory, but it was nearly enough to cheer him up. That was until he caught sight of himself in the broken mirror fixed above the sink. He used to have charisma. He used to be able to smile his way out of trouble. Now he was lucky if people didn't cross the street to avoid him. Greying hair, dull red eyes, pallid skin. He was thirty-three; he looked fifty; he felt like a pensioner. The great Reacher Charlie Smith—reduced to this. Things had changed so radically in just a year. One year, two months, and eight days.

The lock in the front door turned. Charlie straightened his clothes. Everything was normal, everything was fine. He could cope, of course he could cope. He checked his smile in the mirror and stepped out of the bathroom as his brother kicked open the door and then kicked it closed again, to make his point.

"Everything okay?" Charlie asked.

His younger brother wore a scowl so deep it could have been chiselled into his skull. Everything was clearly not okay. But with John it was impossible to tell how far up the disaster scale the situation was. Charlie had seen that same scowl when a job went sour and he'd seen it when someone spilt coffee on John's suit.

"What happened?"

John glanced away. He was annoyed with himself – never a good sign. Charlie braved a crutch-supported step towards him. There was a four year age gap between the two of them, and it had never been more apparent.

Charlie gestured for them to sit down at the fold-up table in the dining space. Most of the time John had everything under control. It was rare for him to make mistakes or miscalculations, and when he did he would beat himself up over it for days. He would need Charlie, a professional in screwing things up, to put everything into perspective.

"She saw me," John confessed.

"She saw you!" Charlie said in disbelief. "You're like a creature of the night, how the hell could see you? Jesus, most of the time I don't even see you and I know you're coming."

John's fists clenched and unclenched. He stood up to work off the tension and started to pace; short, quick steps, squeaking his leather shoes against the linoleum floor.

"There was an explosion. Some bastard left a lure bomb right on her route. I had to pull her away before the goddamn building fell on her."

Charlie pinched the bridge of his nose. Even when his brother messed up he still managed to do something right. "What you mean is you saved her?"

John glared at him. "You're missing the point."

Charlie rolled his eyes. Only John would get himself so worked up over saving the life of their mark. "Listen, do you think he'd pay us if he found out we let her die?" Charlie said.

"You don't know that. We have no idea what he wants her for!"

It was true, they didn't and the fact was starting to chafe. The infamous Smith Brothers always knew the cards on the table before the deck was even dealt. Charlie planned jobs like he was writing a script. Nobody ever missed a cue. At least that was how it used to be a year ago. A year, two months, and eight days. Since then the jobs had dried up. They were lucky to get the Rachel Aaron case and that was only because Charlie's old mentor put in a good word for them. But luck and even the backing of an old priest didn't make the unknown any less troubling. They were out of their depth and they were still only in the shallows.

"Maybe he wants her dead," John stated.

"If he wanted her dead he would have asked us to kill her," Charlie replied. "And if he wanted her dead he wouldn't be approaching a priest to see if he knew anyone who could find her. He wants her found John, that's all."

"I don't like it," John snapped. "This whole job feels off."

"I know." Charlie took a deep breath, his next sentence shouldn't have made him nervous but it did. "Which is why I'm going to do a little field work myself."

John never looked surprised, or happy, or anything other than mildly impatient, but when something pleased him his right eyebrow would lift ever so slightly. As it rose, Charlie felt a pang of guilt that he hadn't said it sooner.

"I thought you were a liability," John jibed.

"It's surveillance in a hospital John, who's going to blend in better, me or you?"

The eyebrow perched higher on John's forehead. He'd been patient with Charlie, more patient than Charlie felt he'd deserved, waiting for his brother to get back in the game instead of going out on his own. John hadn't lost his edge. He didn't have a problem with stairs. He could drink what he wanted. Sleep when he needed. There was nothing wrong with his abilities. Charlie was holding them both back, but he knew John still clung to the hope that one day Charlie would recover and things would go back to normal. And Charlie needed him too much to tell him that was never going to happen.

"You sure about this?" John asked.

"We need the money."

"What if he does want to kill her, or worse?"

Despite what Charlie had said it was always a possibility. They weren't working for the good guys on this one and the girl had been hard to find, even with Charlie's powers. It was not going to end well for her and maybe that was why Charlie hadn't asked enough questions.

"We need the money," Charlie assured him. "That has to be our priority." That wasn't him talking. Sure he'd done questionable things, bad things even, but he had morality and right now it was screaming inside his head that this was all wrong.

John nodded, and Charlie was relieved to see that John was sharing his sentiments. "Fine, but if it has to be done I'll do it."

"No, you don't need this on your conscience. I'll do it."

John gave him a look. "Are we seriously going to argue about who gets to kill her?"

"Has to," Charlie corrected. "When you say 'gets to kill her' you kind of make it sound like a bonus prize. And no, we're not going to argue because I'll do it." He didn't have to say because it was his fault all of this had happened – that was a given.

John folded his arms. "Okay, but I get to dispose of the body."

Charlie scowled. "Did you mean to say 'get to'?"

His brother smirked. He had a unique sense of humour.

3

It took eight years for the British Empire to fall.

Like dominoes, major players in Europe and the western world started to topple, one by one. Each country falling hard enough to ensure the chain reaction was cataclysmic across the globe. Historians disagree where the trouble started; some argue it went as far back as the Second World War when the powers in charge set to picking up the broken pieces of the world and gluing them back together. Others are more cynical, claiming that man was destined towards devastation as soon as the first communities were formed by primitive apes.

However it happened, the cracks had been under the surface for a long, long time, growing weaker and more unstable. Internal conflict kept many countries in a stalemate. Where poverty and war still had a stronghold the effect of what was about to happen would barely touch the Richter scale. But in places like America, France, and Britain, places that had settled comfortably into peace and grown rich from their warring neighbours, the disturbance would be off the charts.

It was the financial crisis that struck the first blow. Each country struggled to balance its homeland cashbook, taking more credit and lending out money until the value of currency plummeted. When the system fell apart civilised government started to crumble, unable to compromise political greed and public integrity. The people revolted, seeing big cats in the big cities squandering money while their families starved in the suburbs. In France and Britain the rioting lasted five years, erupting into a burst of devastating civil war. Places like Red Forest and further north became impassable trenches of conflict that even the militia couldn't conquer.

The civil unrest was brought to a temporary halt when disease started to spread through Yorkshire and Lancashire. Birth deformities, viruses, and contamination concerns separated Britain into two halves and all who could fled south to escape the troubles. Northern Britain was abandoned and even Wales and Cornwall found themselves lost in isolated beacons out of London's reach. Disease spread, terrorism battled prejudice, and before anyone had realised it, aid packets were being flown over from Germany and the Australians were holding rock concerts for British kids in poverty. Most of the country slummed, counties broke off, and suddenly all that anyone seemed to care about was the thriving capital, where business men still wore Armani and sipped espressos. And that was the hardest pill to swallow; despite what was happening less than a hundred miles away, London was still thriving in a modern utopia.

People fled to the great city; their safe haven which grew like a tourniquet around London. Looking to fill the rumoured jobs and sample the last remnants of the good life, most found, when they got there, that London was walled off with wire fences as tall as the buildings they were enclosing. The cops kept watch and if you couldn't pay, you weren't coming in. The gathering crowd clustered and culminated, and eventually Safe Haven, or S'aven as the locals called it, became a city in its own right; a city with rulers as powerful as any of the fat men sitting in parliament square, and just as ruthless.

Pinky Morris had been one of those men, or at least his late brother Frank was. Pinky was more of the Deputy Prime Minster, to cover the summer holidays. They arrived in S'aven, when it was still a town of tents and ramshackle buildings, to sell hooch and marijuana to the refugees. People were starving but they could all afford a couple of joints. Business grew rapidly and one day Pinky blinked and the Morris brothers were at the top of the pecking order with an entire city underneath them. Frank was the boss, all smiles and threats, and Pinky was always there to back his little brother up with brawn and attitude. Together they could do anything. And they did.

That was more than a decade ago, before Pinky lost his empire, lost his respect, lost his brother. He was about to turn fifty-five, he'd lost most of his hair, his stomach was starting to sag, and he was back to running a small drug cartel in the back of his wife's club like he was just approaching twenty. His life had circled and he was pinning everything he had on it starting again.

The walls of his office were plastered with photograph after photograph; a memorial to the good old days. The little frozen moments captured a time Pinky could barely believe had happened. Hundreds of historical faces stared at him from his cramped office at the back of the bar, scrutinising the state he was in. And why wouldn't they, they were from a time when he was on top and meant something in S'aven. Those glossy faces that surrounded him in his youth were gone now, mostly dead or hovering in the vicinity as haggard and as old and as spent as he was. What did they think of him now? It was a question he'd try to avoid asking himself. The answers only ever made him angry. After all it wasn't his fault he was fighting for space at the bottom of the sewers again; he was just a victim of circumstance.

But all of that was about to change. He could feel a ball vibrating in the pit of his stomach. It was ambition and it had been a long time since he'd allowed himself to dream. The depression was almost over.

His eyes fell on the face that occupied every single picture: his brother, Frank. Pinky had tried to change things when he died. He had to. Frank had left them penniless with a reputation as worthless as their bank balance. Pinky had watched Frank's demise, and he had decided to do things differently. He didn't want to rule the city in fear, watching his back in every reflection. He let things slide now and again. He let the Russians move closer to his territory. He went easy on his boys. And he watched as it all came apart. Frank would never have let it happen, Pinky could see that now. His brother wasn't perfect, but he was right for the city. S'aven needed a man like Frank Morris, and Pinky just regretted it had taken him seven sorry years to realise those shoes needed filling, not replacing.

The man sitting opposite him coughed, clearing his throat rather than trying to attract Pinky's attention. He used to be called Donnie Boom and his face was scattered across the wall beside nearly every picture of Frank, not that anyone would recognise him. Most of Donnie's face was melted away, scarred from the explosion seven years ago. Even Pinky had to second guess himself when Donnie first made contact again.

That was four months ago, and Donnie's grey eyeball still made Pinky's stomach churn. But even before the scars, Donnie was enough to give a grown man nightmares. Now he just looked like the monster he had always been inside. And after all this time apart Pinky had forgotten just how crazy his late brother's best friend actually was.

"You blew it up," Pinky stated with impatience. He rapped his fingers against the desk. His nails were bitten to the pinks of his fingers, the skin on his knuckles cracked and sore. They were the hands of an old man.

"I did what needed to be done."

"Under whose authority?"

Donnie eyed Pinky with intense frustration, that grey eyeball pulsating in its scorched socket. "Your brother's. That bitch killed him, she needed to be taught a lesson."

Pinky lifted his thick rimmed glasses and rubbed the tiredness from his eyes. Donnie didn't understand the situation in S'aven anymore, or he just didn't care. Blowing up the most reputable brothel in S'aven was like starting an underground war and he didn't have the man power or the money to fight it. He was beginning to regret allowing Donnie back into the fold despite all that Donnie was promising him.

"You need to lie low for a while."

"I can help with—"

Pinky raised his hand sharply. "You want to fucking help, you keep your bombs out of my city!" Pinky yelled, surprising himself.

He sat back in his chair and stared at Donnie. His temper was starting to get the better of him these days. He couldn't remember Frank ever yelling. He never had to; Frank commanded respect without it.

Pinky calmed himself and lowered his voice. "Enough buildings are going up around this place without you helping. People are going to be asking about you now, Donnie. My people are going to be asking about you."

"Then let them know I'm back. I don't get all this cloak and dagger shit."

"You don't get it. You put a bomb under my brother's table and blew him half way across S'aven!"

"I didn't mean to kill them. I told you, the instructions were from Frank's phone. I was set up."

"Exactly and you want the people who set you up on to us, do you? Whoever it was I want them with their guard down, do you understand me? You stay off the grid and don't come around here anymore. I'll call you when I need you."

"What about when you get the girl?"

"I'll call you. Once we have her, we have everything. But we have to play this carefully, Donnie. Frank pissed off a lot of people. We can't just assume it was Lulu Roxton that killed him. When we have the girl, we'll know."

Donnie nodded. He was crazy but he wasn't stupid.

"I appreciate what you're doing," he said running what was left of his hand through his matted red hair. "You didn't have to believe me."

"You took a risk coming back here, I figured you were either suicidal or telling the truth," Pinky told him.

"I had to," Donnie assured him. "I have to know who did it, Pinky. I loved Frank. What they made me do to him..." Donnie shook his head, close to crying – it was an unsettling sight. "You're right, I shouldn't be here. Sometimes it's hard for me to think. My head gets kind of messed up, from the explosion. I'll get out of your way."

He reached the door before he turned around. "You remember you said I'd get to finish them?"

Pinky nodded; he did remember. With that, Donnie left. There was no way Pinky was going to let some deranged, half mad pyromaniac finish anything.

"What did he want?" Pinky's wife stood in the open doorway.

"Revenge," Pinky replied.

Riva swayed into the room. For a woman in her forties she was still turning heads. She smiled at Pinky, it was a natural smile, unblemished by silicone and cosmetics like the rest of the wives he knew. Sometimes Pinky would look at her and wonder what the hell she was still doing with him. He wondered if she asked herself the same question.

"Any news on the girl?"

"They think they have her."

"Do you want me to send someone to get her?" The question set Pinky on edge. He still had men, not as many as the old days, but there was still an entourage. Only now his wife had her own money from the club and she was investing it all in a legal security firm which was making his own boys look like school kids. Using them would be better, but they were Riva's boys, Riva's bodyguards, Riva's heavies, Riva's assassins. Not his. He didn't like it.

Pinky shook his head. "I'm going to send a couple of the old guys." He didn't say 'my' guys for her benefit.

"What about those brothers?"

"We'll deal with them when she's safely locked away. This time it's going to be different, Riva. I'm going to get my city back."

Dear reader,

We hope you enjoyed reading Family. Please take a moment to leave a review, even if it's a short one. Your opinion is important to us.

Discover more books by L.E. Fitzpatrick at
https://www.nextchapter.pub/authors/le-fitzpatrick-science-fiction-author

Want to know when one of our books is free or discounted for Kindle? Join the newsletter at
http://eepurl.com/bqqB3H

Best regards,

L.E. Fitzpatrick and the Next Chapter Team

ABOUT THE AUTHOR

L E Fitzpatrick is a writer of dark adventure stories and thrillers. Under the watchful eye of her beloved rescue Staffordshire bull terrier, she leaps from trains and climbs down buildings, all from the front room of a tiny cottage in the middle of the Welsh countryside.

Inspired by cult film and TV, L E Fitzpatrick's fiction is a collection of twisted worlds and realities, broken characters, and high action. She enjoys pushing the boundaries of her imagination and creating hugely entertaining stories.

www.lefitzpatrick.com

Lightning Source UK Ltd.
Milton Keynes UK
UKHW011857040221
378281UK00010B/490/J